TIME MACHINE

RAW VERSION

YOGENDRA NIKALE

at the end the parents watches the shadow of the man and the woman and the daughter.

written by : yogendra nikale
tittle : time machine

in a old mansion
professor egor is in late 40s, he has a bread and long hair, and few of his hair are grey.
professor egor wakes up from his bed and watches the clock the is ticking and the pendulum is hanging. he watches his marraige picture hanging on the wall and his daughters picture too. suddenly the alarm starts ringing from the clock. [close up shot of the eyes]
egor wears the sleepers under his bed and goes in the bathroom. he wants everything to be perfect. he wears his clothes in front of the mirror and watches at her daughter and child photograph, and exits the room.
egor sits in the dinning table and waits for his break fast, the spoon on the table is not set properly, he sets them properly. he watches dirt on the napkin. he twiches it. he watches the window is opened he goes and closes it
butler comes on the table with the braek fast.
egor takes the napkin and tugs in under his collar.
butler gives the news paper to the egor.
butler : the newspaper.
egor : why the news paper, im not interested in the outside world
butler : this season there is going to be more storms . schools and colleges will be announcing holidays for a week.
egor : so what i got to do with it.
butler : sir, i might need some holidays to fix the roof top. the storm

might destroy my house.
egor : who will do the job here when you go. you are getting paid in full aint you.
butler : yes sir.
egor : so keep doing what your doing. or leave this job and be i your house forever. anyways there is still time for the stor, you can still fix it after the office hours.
the phone rings. and egor watches the break fast. he takes spoon in his hand and the butler speaks
butler : sir its your parents.
egor : do you really dont know what to say.
butler on the phone : sir just left the house.
egor cuts the omlet from the knife. and butler speaks.
butler : sir your parents just gave a message, they wanted to wish you happy birthday, they just want tto speak with you once.
egor yells : why dont you do your job as told, the nakin has dirt on it, the spoon are not placed properly, the windows are open to pass the dirt in. do your job instead of giving me stupid messages.
egor : its been years i didnt had a decent breakfast in this house [egor gets up takes his bag and heads out and butler looks down the phone rings again]
egor while leaving : dont pick up, its them again let it ring
on the other side of the phone mother is holding the phone.
mother to father : he is not picking up
father : its been years we havent spoke to him.
mother : he havent forgotten his past yet. he should forgive himself.
egor goes out he watches a girl is throwing stones at the tree in his compound to get a fruit from the tree.
egor : why you little devil, go and plant your own tree so you can throw stones on it.
egor walking down the street there is a lady selling ice cream and she

a bell on it. as watching egor she stops the bell,
eggor to the lady : why dont you bring the church bell to sell you icecream
children playing socker on the street, the ball passes over his head and he ducks.
egor to childre : you orphan rats, you cannot afford school so took over the street. next you will be killing in dark for money. get lost you insects to the society.
begger is on the street
egor to the beggar : this footpath is made so we can walk.
egor was crossing the street and car comes in speed, as it passes egor yell watch where your going hotwheels.
as egor enters the school gate all the children from the school gets silence.
egor getting in staff room everyone gets silenced and starts making faces that he has come.
egor taking lecture in the college of science and evryone is is silenced, one girl pases a letter to the boyfriend, the boyfriend reads canteen after the lecture and they bot smiles and egor throws chawk at her.
egor in principles ooffice
principle to the girl : you may leave now.
the girl leaves from the office and meets her boyfriend,
boyfriend : what hapened.
girl : i said what happened, this college is so nice. except this rotten tomatto.
principle to egor : throwing chawks on students is not done in this school.
egor : there should be decipline in the classrom, students suppose to concentrate, they have future, they should do the right thing, study, work, safety of family,watchout for small things and even they should drive safely wih their seat belts on. [hearing this principle eyes in tears

]
principle : egor you are good to go. [egor leaves]
principle turn his chair towards the window and starts crying .
egor goes back home, and enters the project room. and inside he keeps on working with gajets.
butler knocks the door and egor opens.
butler : sir the dinnner is on the table, good night and about the holiday [egor shuts the door and behind the door he is standing and hearing the foot step of butler and looks at his project.
butler goes home
butlers wife : how was your way back home [give coffee from a tea pot in cup]
butler : the road is still the same, just we have gotten old.
butlers wife : did you speak to him,
butler : to whom.
butler's wife : you know what im talking about.
butler : holiday is impossible, dad by day the darkness is consuming him, he has stopped eating his breakfast also. he is dying very slowly, [both crying]i cannot see his end this way.
butler's wife : he is not letting the past go, he still rmembers them [both hugs and cry]
butler : [cryingly] everyday my love , everyday.
egor in the shop of electronics bying stufffrom his list.
the shp keeper : we have all the stuff, exceppt this liqiud acids
egor : this is equipment shop aint it.
the shop keeper : yes but, the amount which you need we cannot provide, no one can.
egor : im a science teacher, i need this stuff, im not making a bomb out of it.
the shopkeeper : im sorry sir, the only place you are gonna get this amount is in your college stock.

egor starts stealing the liqiud acids from the college lab.
the students were practicing with chemicals in science lab and even the girl
the girl went to help to her boyfriend, while helping looked at her table thate egor was standing therre with his metal bottle and she continues helping him again. aafter helping she goes to her desk, she find that her chemicals are missing and the professor had also disapeared from there.
she gets suspicious of him and she watches him all the time and his bag during the lecture.
she speaks to her boyfriend after class : i think the professor is hiding something from us.
boyfriend : ye he is hiding his demon inside him.
girl ; dont talk rubbish, i think he is upto something. he is stealing chemicals from the lab.
boyfriend : you are saying this because, you just hate him.
girl : its not that, [professor walks in front of them] look how he walks, he is always hidding something.
the boyfriends friends calls him soccer ground in 5mins.
boyfriend to his friends : i will be there. [then to his girl] listen feel free to solve this mystery, some of us have goals to kick [and runs towards different direction]
girl : i will find whats he up to.
the girl follows him till his house and she figures out where he lives.
she reaches home and calls her boyfriend.
boyfriend : hey mystery girl, did you figure out where the chemicals went.
girl : listen i figured out where he lives.
boyfriend : what ? you follow him. dont you think you are taking this too far.
girl : meet me after dinner, lets checkout his house.

boyfriend : we will get in trouble, police may get us for trespassing.

girl : only if we get caught.

boyfriend : im not doing this, you are onn your own.

girl : what a pussy ur, its ok you dont come.

boyfriend : you are not gonna stop arent you

girl : no.

boyfriend : ok, i will pick you up around 9, be ready.

girl : and listen, i love you my pussy.

boyfriend : after tonight, you will call my a tiger. lets do this. but remember if we get caught we will be arested for trespassing.

the girl watches the wall and on the clock its its 5 and time lapse till

9

the boy comes on the bike outside the girls house and the girl hops on the bike.

boyfriend : why is the bag for

girl : i told my parents we are doing a group study, i will be late.

the boy reaches the house and the girl says stop thats the house.

the boy parks the bike away from the house and removes the gloves from his pocket,

girl : what this for.

boyfriend : i watched it on television. for safety of our fingerprints.

girl : so smart, you should choose breaking into house as profession [while enetering the house gate]

boyfriend : shut up im doing this for you, this is the first and the last time.[the buttler comes out from the main door they hide in the bushes watching him.]

girl ; who is he

boyfriend ; i thinkk, he might be a servant or something.

the butler exits from the gate and they come out of the bushhes and comes close towards the house, they check the main door its unable to open.

boyfriend : lets check if there is any other way. [they rotates around
the house and they find a window open. and they eneter inside]
the lights are off in the hall near the dinning table. the boyfriend
turns on the flashlight.
giirl : what are you doing,
boyfrend : i dont have powers to see in the dark.
they check around the house in the bedroom and everywhere they
wattch the photo of his wife and dauughter.
girl : lovely girl [watching the photo]
boyfriend : look the man is married. [watching the photo]
girl : but there is no one in the house.
boyfriend : its not a surprise, who will live with such a man, now come
llets get out here before someone catches us.
girl : but where is the professor.[suddenly a sound comes from a
room of some machine the girl watches in the room from the key
hole.]
girl : i told you he was up to something.
boyfriend : let me watch [now he watches from the kcy hole]
girl watches there is a ventilator window on the top of the wall but
she couldnt reach it
girl : i need a clear view,
boyfriend : how its possible.
girl : just trust me.
butler on the street walking and he remembers that he didnt close
the window. so he heads back towards the house.
the girl is climbing on the boys shoulder and the vent grill falls down
inside but egor doesnt notices
boyfriend : what are you doing.
girl : just stand still he didnt even notived, the machinery is too loud.
the girl watches there different motor and clocks around the room,
some chemicals flowing in different tubes of different colours a circle

in between and on the top of the circle there are 2 giant electric bolts
and she watches his family photo on the top of the black board and
black baord there is written E equals to MC square. with lot of
scriblings.
girl : i knew he was into something, but i never thought of time travel.
boyfriend : do you know how heavy you are, you got what you came
for come down now. [sudenly torch light on his face , he watches the
light and a rod strikes on the boys head he falls and the girl falls
down.]
girl : please dont hurt us, we are not burglars, we are students
[crawling backwards and flashlight on her face of a torch and she
removes her bag and shows her id]
butler : students, [the butler stops coming forward and goes near
the switch board and turns on the light] may i ask what are you doing
here.
girl : we were suspicious about the professor. what is he upto. [she
tries to wake up the boy]
butler : dont worry, he will be up in few minutes.
girl : what is happening here, and what is he doing.
butler : dont read the dark pages of his book. leave him alone, there
are only pages left of his life.
girl ; why does he want to do time travel.
butler : clever girl, you figured it out. if i tell you promise me you will
keep his act a secret.
girl : a promise.
butler : but not here he might come out any moment drag him to the
front room its the kitchen.
the girl drags the boy till the kitchen and she watches there is knife.
girl : can i get some water.
butler : sure [he goes to get the water and she takes the knife and
hides it behind her back.]

butler : take the chair, [comes with the water]
she takes the sip of the water, keeps the glass, takes the chair and sits watshes the boy and then the butler
girl : what is this madness of this rude guy.
butler : rude guy, he was the loved once of everyone. even in your college.
girl : dont lie, everyone hates him there.
butler : yes, i know but he started drowing from past 10 years before that he was a happy guy.
he was married to a wonderfull girl, stephany she was an art teacher in your college
they both were very happy together. [they both eating in staff room of college and offering other teachers as well, all the teachers watching them. they talk among themselves they look so good together]
they both had a daughter angel. she was an real angel [shots of angel playing and going to church with the famiily and playing football with egor as well]
angel : dad today i heard about einstein.
egor : what you heard about, his stolen brain.
angel : no, his equation. E equals to MC square,
egor : its a time travel.
angel : yes, so if you go back in time, you can alert people, so you can save so many lives.
egor : yes ofcourse, but who will make such a gajet.
angel : you know science, right. so its your responsibility to save the people.
egor : my little angel wants to save the planet. who is going to save you from this tiger now [starts ticking her belly and she is lughing]
butler : this is a stormy area, whenever there is a storm, egor used to go to his parents house and pray together for every living soul [

visuals]
butler : but there was night which haunts him every night.
cut to
egor driving the car and there is strong storm, his wife is sitting next to him and his kid is sitting on the back seat.
wife : the storm was gonna start in the morning, how it started now.
angel : im afraid dady [crying]
egor : dont worry darling, daddy is here for you.[watching back and telling angel]
egor to wife : i dont know, sometime we cannot predict the nature.
wife : can you see the road.
egor : the wind and the rain is blocking my view, i think we should have stayed home this time.
angel crying loudly.
wife : dont worry my child. come to me.
egor : no, if you take her in front you both will loose the seat belts,
angel : please mamma take me.
wife : please let her come to me, she is afraid, and god is with us, he wont let the storm hurt us.
egor : ok but make it quick.
angel comes in front oseat on the lap of the wife
egor : angel my preety girl, daddy is dont you worry. i am always with you, my love.
angel : promise.
egor : i promise, my angel [and the car blows i the storm]
cut ot butler
butler in tears : egor survived and both the angels died, sometimes god isnt fair. i heard he works in different ways, but this was not the way. he thinks it was his mistake, he never should have let them unpluck the seat belts.
girl is also in tears.

butlers naration : when he recovered from his injuries he came home,
for many days he didnt poke to anyone,he used to get sleepless
nights [crying in room and getting sleepless nights and visionns of
the storm night visuals]
buttler : he stopped praying, he stoped talking to his parents because
they believed in god[visuals in room alone and butler behind him and
parents are outside his door calling his name and to open the door.]
butler : and one night he reminded what his girl said about time
travel. and from that day he only thinks of time travel. any sound or
any interference distracts him and he gets angry. because there is
always one thought in the mind. he is not rude he is just stuck
somewhere from past few years. [visuals of egor was thinking in the
staff room getting distracted in staffroom and telling taechers to
keep silence and even the type writer. on the streets also]
butler : and from that day till today he only works on his project. [
visual working from scrach to the equiment he has built till the day
and even his beard time lapse]
cut to butler : and im worried how it ends.
girl crying and wiping her tears [and the engine stops]
butler : he had stopped working, i have to stop him there, as goes to
his bedroom, you and your boy go from here.
egor opens the door and sits onn the table and the butler enters the
dinners.
egor : alfred you are still here.
butler : yes, i was feeling my age upon me. so i decided to stay
here.[egor opens the cover plate from the food and starts eating]
egor : did you had dinner [girl watching from the kitchen hiding behind
the wall]
butler : after you sir.
egor : now dont ask me to serve you.
butler sits on the dinning table and starts eating

butler : sir there is no salt , why didnt you say so sir [egor is eating and girl watching him crying]

egor : this end tomorrow alfred , this ends tomorrow.

next day the girl is watching, egor when he is teaching and she also goes through the history of the teachers she finds about steffanny.

and in the science lab the boy and the girl are next to each other.

boyfriend : what happened last night, how did i got subconciuos, do u have anything to explain.

girl : you fel and i draged you to the kitchen room, i woke you up and we came home. and lets not talk about last night.

boyfriend : what ? that man is up to something, you saw with your own eyes. dont you think we have to tell somme one.

girl : tell what, we broke into his house, we might go to jail. just let things go.

there is a blast of some experiment of a student and everyone geos towards it and as they come back the boys liquid chemicals are missing.

the boy calls the lab incharge and tell him his chemicals are stolen and claims that the egor has taken it and kept it in his steel water bottle. and he is up to something.

egor : if you reallly think that your chemicals in this bottle, so i will drink in front of you.

girl : no sir, there has been a mistake, i took his chemicals.

boy : what are you sayiing. why are you saving him.

girl : thats the truth, take your chemicals back and shut this nonsense.

and everyone gets back to their chair and starts working.

butler says good night as usual to egor

egor : i dont know whats gonna happen, but you take care of your self.

egor shuts the door.

alfred reaches home
alfred : he is gonna do the experiment tonight.
wife : if it didnt work.
butler : he will keep trying until he dies.
wife : ohh lord, what will happen to us if we loose him. there will be
no income. [watches her grandchildren sleeping]
butler : everyone has to die one day, even our roof may colapse, last
storm has weaken it. one more storm it will fall. we still have 2 days
we can fix it.
wife : just keep in mind we lost our children. i dont want to loose my
grandchildren now.
butler : i dont think this roof will last long. ill try my best to fix it
[alfred fixing the roof from the top.]
wife : god give us strenth to face this disaster, give me strenth to
protect my family and let egor get what he is looking for, he is a good
man he is just in too much of pain, i cannot see him suffer more,
release the man from his pain. [egor starting the experiment and the
girl entering the house and watching rom the window]
the machine starts the clock stars ticking all the machines starts
working the chemicals traveling to the tubes, and the top bolts
started rotating. andd the electric lightening all over. and egor stands
in the center of the circle and the lightening starts touching him.
suddenly the clock starts leaving smoke, the experiment is now gonna
blast, and every object starts getting destroyed from fire and even
the bolt, he gets a big shock and falls on the away from the blast.
egor is on the floor and opens his eyes in the same room but the
room is different there no equipments . he watches his wife
wife : get up honey, you have come a long way.
he watches and gets stunned, his girl comes near him. he gets up and
he hugs her.
angel : what a mess you look daddy.

egor : oh my lovely daughter, i missed you my baby, dont leave me
again. listen to papa this time.
angel : you listen to me now. its not your time yet to be here. you still
have to go back
egor : what are you saying, i cannot live without you, i miss you.
angel : im always around you, im everywhere. you hurt anyone you
hurt me.
egor : this cannot happen.
wife : come here honey, i know you havent slept a single night
properly. [she takes him on her lap an the daughter comes closer]
angel : i was wrongg dady, its not your resposibility to time travel, its
your responsibility to keep everyone happy.
egor opens his eyes [top shot] and the girl is next to him. the
equipment is destroyed and there are little parrticles of the machine
around him in fire.
girl : are you ok sir,
egor : [choughing] yes im fine, what are you doing here.
girl : i know everything about you sir, alfred told me every thing.
egor : so it was you last night, not the burglars.
girl : you knew there were people in the house.
egor : i do have ears and eyes, [he shows the went grill] but at that
moment, the only thing was important was the experiment.
girl : im so sorry, i will help you to rebuild it.
egor : no need, my child, i got my answers.
next day butler comes in the house.
he watches the equipments is blowed up and little bit of smoke and
he watches egor cleaning all the mess from the house.
butler : egor, wait its my job. you step a side.
egor : ohh your right, alfred the storm is coming in 2 days, so we have
lot of things to do, we have to remove all this stuff and make it brand
news again.

butler : sir, but i have to fix my house roof before the storm.
egor : no need, your family is moving here. with us.
butler : sir, are you serious.
egor : yes alfred, do it before i change my mind [wearing the coat and going towards the door]
butler : sir what hapened last night.
egor : the machine worked alfred..[and he goes outside]
egor watches the girl throwing stones on the tree to grab the fruit.
egor : dont know how to aim and throw. [the girl gets shocked] wait i will show you.
egor throws the stone on the tree and a fruit falls. he takes the fruit and gives it to her. the girl smilles.
egor : keep practicing my child, keep practicing. [and walks away from there]
he walks down the street a lady is selling ice cream. after watching him she stop her bell. he goes near her as he is angry.
egor : how much your entire ice cream cost.
lady : [scared] huh huh. im sorry professor.
egor : [removes a bundle of money from his pocket and shows her] is this amount enough.
lady : yes, its enough.
egor : [gives the money to the lady and she also takes in fear and egor holds the bell and shouts] ice cream ice cream free ice cream, [it gets crowded there]
egor to lady : you realy dont know how to sell your ice cream. [egor exits from the crowd]
walks further and watches the drunkk beggar. he was drinking. egor comes near his face.
egor : what are you drinking.
beggar : brandy from down the road.
egor : you beg the entire day and this what you are drinking. come by

the house, you are going to have scotch from every day.[egor walks
away from there and the beggar watches him going and itches his
head. the car was pasing by and egor stops and he bends and syas
after you sir, and the beggar smells is confused and smells the
alcohol thinking is it the alcohol or the professor have gone mad]
there are children playing on the street one boy kicks and the ball
heads towards egor.
egor : why you little rats. dont you know tthat the storm is in 3 days,
streets are not safe for you anymore, come with me to my house you
will not live on streets anymore.
in the coollege staffroom egor enters and every gets silence. and even
to type writer stops typing.
egor : this silence is killing me. [everyone looks at him], at least you
do some typing.
the typist smiles and one of the teacher says its good to have you
back egor.
cleaning in the house alfred and his family, orphans helping egor and
the beggar ordering them and there come the girl with the boyfriend.
they start cleaning. girl calling her boyfriend tiger after he lifts heavy
metals while cleaning.
then painting all together. eating food together. ice cream lady
coming with the ice cream sticks for everyone.
distribution of food
as the cleaning and painting is done there are beds for the orphans
as the work is done egor tells alfred and everyone are behind him.
egor : the work is done here, tomorrow is the storm. everything is upt
to you guys now.
alfred : where are you going.
egor : im missing something, i have to reach somewhere. [alfred exits
the frame]
everone in the room please dont go, please dont.

alfred comes with the his coat and says : drive safe sir.
egor nods and goes starts the car and hits the road.
the storm starts. the kid was in the window, he yells : storm has
started.
alfred : ohh egor, god help you.
egor is driving in the storm. and everyone are praying for him.
the storm is distroying the city. thunders rain and wind.
everyone are praying.
alfred's old house also gets destroyed in the storm.
egor's parents are also prayiing.
egor in the car, having difficulties. he removes his seat belt and says i
believe in you god.
the storm blows his car away.
the parents are praying and suddenly they hear a knock mother
opens she watches egor, tears in her eyes and she hugs egor. tgey sit
together start praying.
and in the egor's house beggar is on the chair sleeping. alfred in his
room with wife. girl with her boyfriend in the kitchen and in the
experiment room everyone are sleeping on the bed and camera pan
till the family photo.
the end

written by yogendra nikale

Contents